7557779

E Marshall, James
Ma.

George and Martha rise
and shine

	MAR 30	MAR 17	JAN 18	JAN 23
			JUN -4	OCT 14	OCT 25	NOV 23
		MAR 27			NOV 14	MAR 06	MAY 02
OCT 20		NOV 08		NOV 26	MAY 25
OCT 13	MAR 25		MAR 27	MAY 25
FEB 28	FEB 05	OCT 30	JUN 10	JUN 07
NOV 23				
MAY 08				

GEORGE AND MARTHA RISE AND SHINE

JAMES MARSHALL

HOUGHTON MIFFLIN COMPANY BOSTON

FOR MY FATHER

Library of Congress Cataloging in Publication Data

Marshall, James, 1942-
George and Martha rise and shine.

SUMMARY: Five brief episodes about two friends,
George and Martha, who happen to be hippopotamuses.
1. Friendship—Fiction. 2. Hippopotamus—Fiction.
3. Short Stories   I. Title
PZ7.M35672Ge   E   76-14350
ISBN 0-395-24738-1   RNF ISBN 0-395-28006-0 PaP

Copyright © 1976 by James Marshall

Printed in the United States of America

Y   10   9   8   7   6   5

ABOUT
TWO FINE FRIENDS

STORY NUMBER ONE

THE FIBBER

One day George wanted to impress Martha.

"I used to be a champion jumper," he said.

Martha raised an eyebrow.

"And," said George, "I used to be a wicked pirate."

"Hmmm," said Martha.

George tried harder. "Once I was even a famous snake charmer!"

"Oh, goody," said Martha.

Martha went to the closet and got out Sam.

"Here's a snake for you to charm."

"Eeeek," cried George.

And he jumped right out of his chair.

"It's only a toy *stuffed* snake," said Martha. "I'm surprised a famous snake charmer is such a scaredy-cat."

"I told some fibs," said George.

"For shame," said Martha.

"But you can see what a good jumper I am," said George.

"That's true," said Martha.

Martha was in her laboratory.

"What are you doing?" asked George.

"I'm studying fleas," said Martha.

"Cute little critters," said George.

"You don't understand," said Martha.

"This is serious. This is science."

The next day, George noticed that Martha was scratching a lot. She looked uncomfortable.

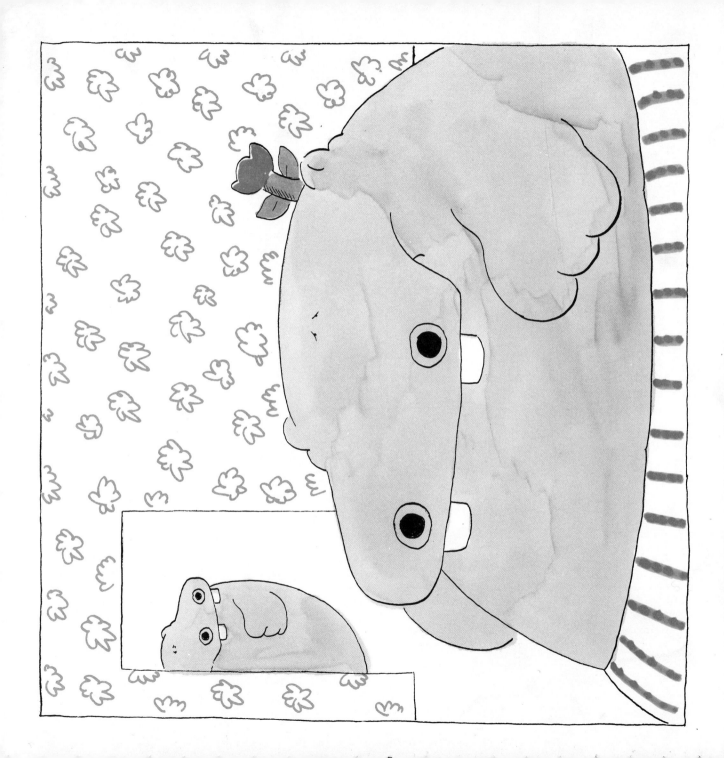

George bought Martha some special soap. After her shower Martha felt much better.

"I think I'll stop studying fleas," said Martha.

"Good idea," said George.

"I think I'll study bees instead," said Martha.

"Oh dear," said George.

One Saturday morning, George wanted to sleep late.

"I love sleeping late," said George.

But Martha had other ideas.

She wanted to go on a picnic.

"Here she comes!" said George to himself.

Martha did her best to get George out of bed.

"Picnic time!" sang Martha.

But George didn't budge.

Martha played a tune on her saxophone.

George put little balls of cotton in his ears and
pulled up the covers.

Martha tickled George's toes.

"Stop it!" said George.

"Picnic time!" sang Martha.

"But I'm *not* going on a picnic." said George.

"Oh yes you *are*!" said his friend.

Martha had a clever idea.

"This is such hard work," she said, huffing and puffing.

"But I'm not going to help," said George.

"I'm getting tired," said Martha.

George had fun on the picnic.

"I'm so glad we came," said George.

But Martha wasn't listening.

She had fallen asleep.

Martha was nervous.

"I've never been to a scary movie before."

"Silly goose," said George. "*Everyone* likes scary movies."

"I hope I don't faint," said Martha.

Martha *liked* the scary movie. "This is fun," she giggled.

Martha noticed that George was hiding under his seat.

"I'm looking for my glasses," said George.

"You don't wear glasses," said Martha.

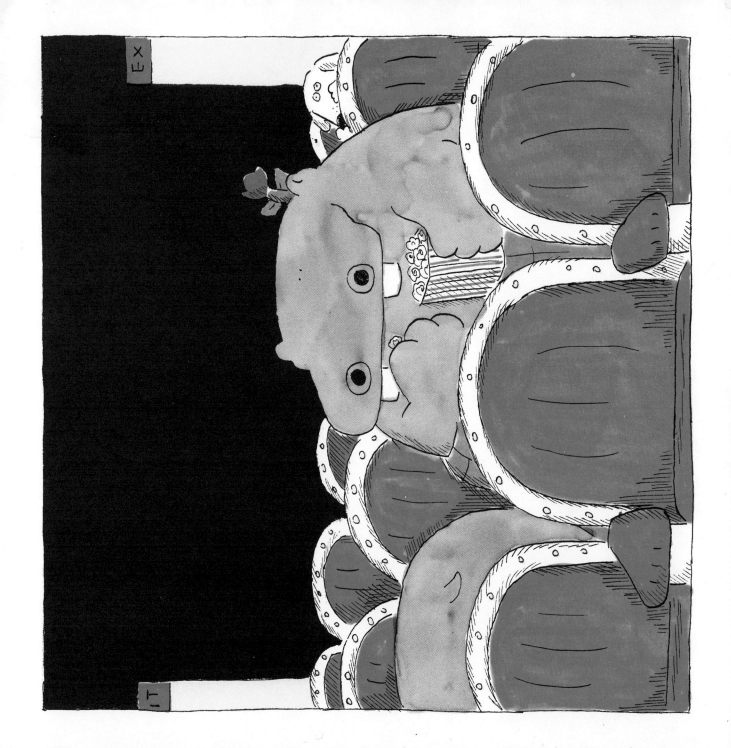

When the movie was over, George was as white as a sheet.

"Hold my hand," George said to Martha. "I don't want you to be afraid walking home."

"Thank you," said Martha.

"Where are you going, George?" asked Martha.

"I'm going to my secret club," said George.

"I'll come along," said Martha.

"Oh no," said George, "it's a secret club."

"But you can let *me* in," said Martha.

"No I can't," said George. And he went on his way.

Martha was furious.

When George was inside his secret clubhouse, Martha made a terrible fuss.

"You let me in," she shouted.

"No," said George.

"Yes, yes," cried Martha.

"No, no," said George.

"I'm coming in whether you like it or *not!*" cried Martha.

When Martha saw the inside of George's clubhouse, she was so ashamed.

"You old sweetheart," she said to George.

George smiled. "I hope you've learned your lesson."

"I certainly have," said his friend.

DATE			

$14.95   04/25/2000

I wonder what I'll be when I grow up.

Grown-ups sure have interesting work to do!
And so do we.

Today it's Mr. Siscoe's turn
to introduce his special visitor.
He says, "Good morning, everyone.
I'd like you to meet Professor Alcorn.
He's my teacher at college."
Hey—I never knew grown-ups
had teachers, too!

When it's time for Nicholas
to introduce his visitor, he says,
"I'll bet you've all bought groceries
at the Friendly Farm Market.
Guess what—my father is manager of the store."

Evan's father wears a leather apron
that holds the tools he uses all the time.
He shows us how to hammer a nail.

Sam's visitor drives the sanitation truck
that carries our garbage to the big town dump.
Kate and Eveline and I wave to him, just as
we always do whenever he comes down our street.
"Hey, kids—remember to recycle!" Sam's father says.

Jessica's mother takes care of animals. She's a veterinarian, the kind of doctor who makes sick animals better.

Eveline's mother is a nurse in the hospital.
She takes care of all the newborn babies in our town.
She tells us those babies are very, very cute,
but they sure do cry a lot when they're hungry.

Sarah's visitor is our crossing guard.
She brings Sarah to school every day,
because she is also Sarah's grandmother.
That's why Sarah is always the first one at school
and the last one to go home in the afternoon.

Mrs. Madoff's visitor is her husband.
He's a scientist called a paleontologist.
He just got back from South America,
where he was digging for dinosaur bones.
The bones tell us about dinosaurs
that lived long ago.

Michiko's mother writes books for us to read.
She draws the pictures in them, too.
She is very good at drawing mice.

When Kate introduces her visitor, she says,
"My dad plays bass in an orchestra at night.
He practices all day and takes care of
my baby brother while our mother goes
to work at the bank."

Next we meet Charlie's visitor.
His mother is a judge who works
in a courtroom and wears a long black robe.
If there's too much noise, she pounds her gavel
and says, "Order in the court!"
Then everyone has to be quiet.

Here he is—right on time!
"Uh, this is my dad," I say.
"He drives a big bulldozer.
He's helping build our new library."
"Good morning, Mr. Lopez," everyone says.
"Good morning, boys and girls," my dad says.

What if I forget what I'm supposed to say?
Sometimes that happens.
Not just to me, Mrs. Madoff says,
but to everyone.

Sam JUICE

Charlie LIGHTS

Kate PLANTS

Pablo FLUFFY

Sarah MAIL

Jessica CALENDAR

Michiko LEADER

Nicholas WEATHER

Eveline SNACK

Evan

When special visitors come to our school,
they tell us about the work they do.
Then we tell them about the work we do.
Today it's my turn to introduce my visitor.

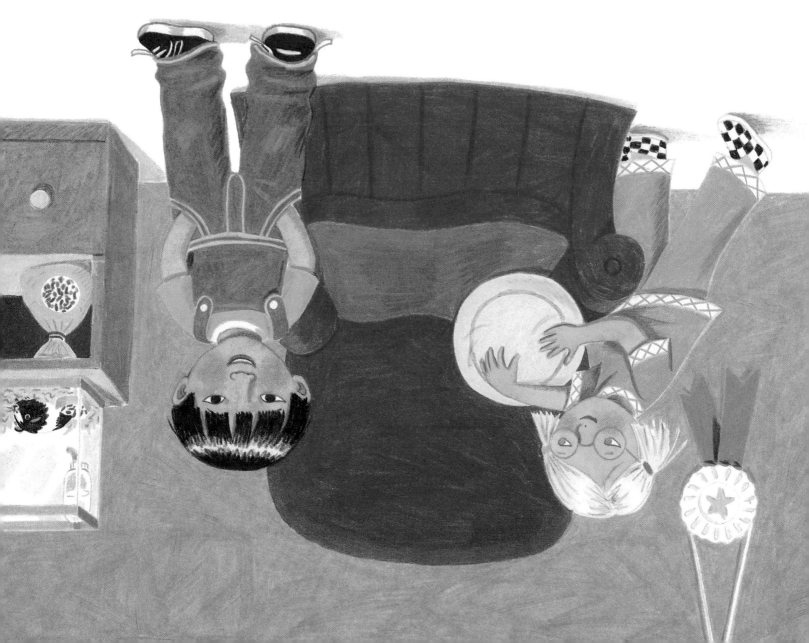

For Christian and Sam,
who will grow up to do something wonderful.
—A.R. and L.R.

Career Day

story by **Anne Rockwell**   pictures by **Lizzy Rockwell**

HarperCollinsPublishers

Career Day • Text copyright © 2000 by Anne Rockwell • Illustrations copyright © 2000 by Lizzy Rockwell • Printed in the U.S.A. All rights reserved.
Visit our web site at http://www.harperchildrens.com. • Library of Congress Cataloging-in-Publication Data • Rockwell, Anne F. • Career day / story by
Anne Rockwell ; pictures by Lizzy Rockwell.   p.   cm.   Summary: Each child in Mrs. Madoff's class brings a visitor who tells the group about his or
her job.   ISBN 0-06-027565-0. — ISBN 0-06-027566-9 (lib. bdg.)   [1. Schools—Fiction. 2. Occupations—Fiction.]   I. Rockwell, Lizzy, ill. II. Title.
PZ7.R5943 Car   2000   97-20999   [E]—DC21   CIP AC   Typography by Elynn Cohen 1 2 3 4 5 6 7 8 9 10 ❖ First Edition